THE AMAZING ADVENTURES OF SUPERMAN!

Bubble Trouble!

by Benjamin Bird

illustrated by Tim Levins

Superman created by Jerry Siegel and Joe Shuster
by special arrangement with the Jerry Siegel family

PICTURE WINDOW BOOKS
a capstone imprint

The Amazing Adventures of Superman
is published by Picture Window Books
a Capstone Imprint
1710 Roe Crest Drive
North Mankato, Minnesota 56003
www.capstonepub.com

STAR34622

Cataloging-in-Publication Data is available at the Library of Congress website.
ISBN: 978-1-4795-6520-7 (library binding)
ISBN: 978-1-4795-6524-5 (paperback)
ISBN: 978-1-4795-8460-4 (eBook)

Summary: SUPERMAN and AQUAMAN defend the skies and the seas in a winning
combination of teamwork and friendship. When Black Manta engineers an evil device
that creates giant bubbles of ocean water capable of flooding entire cities, they'll join
forces and fight as one. In order to save the Metropolis and cities around the globe,
SUPERMAN and AQUAMAN will have to solve this . . . Bubble Trouble!

Designer: Bob Lentz

Printed and bound in the USA.
009397R

TABLE OF CONTENTS

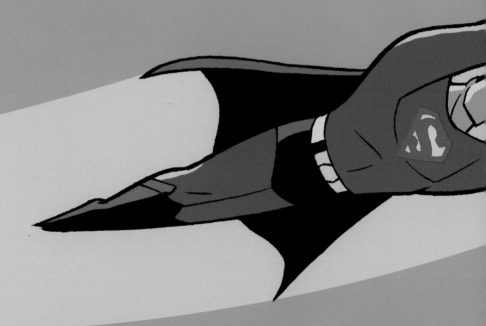

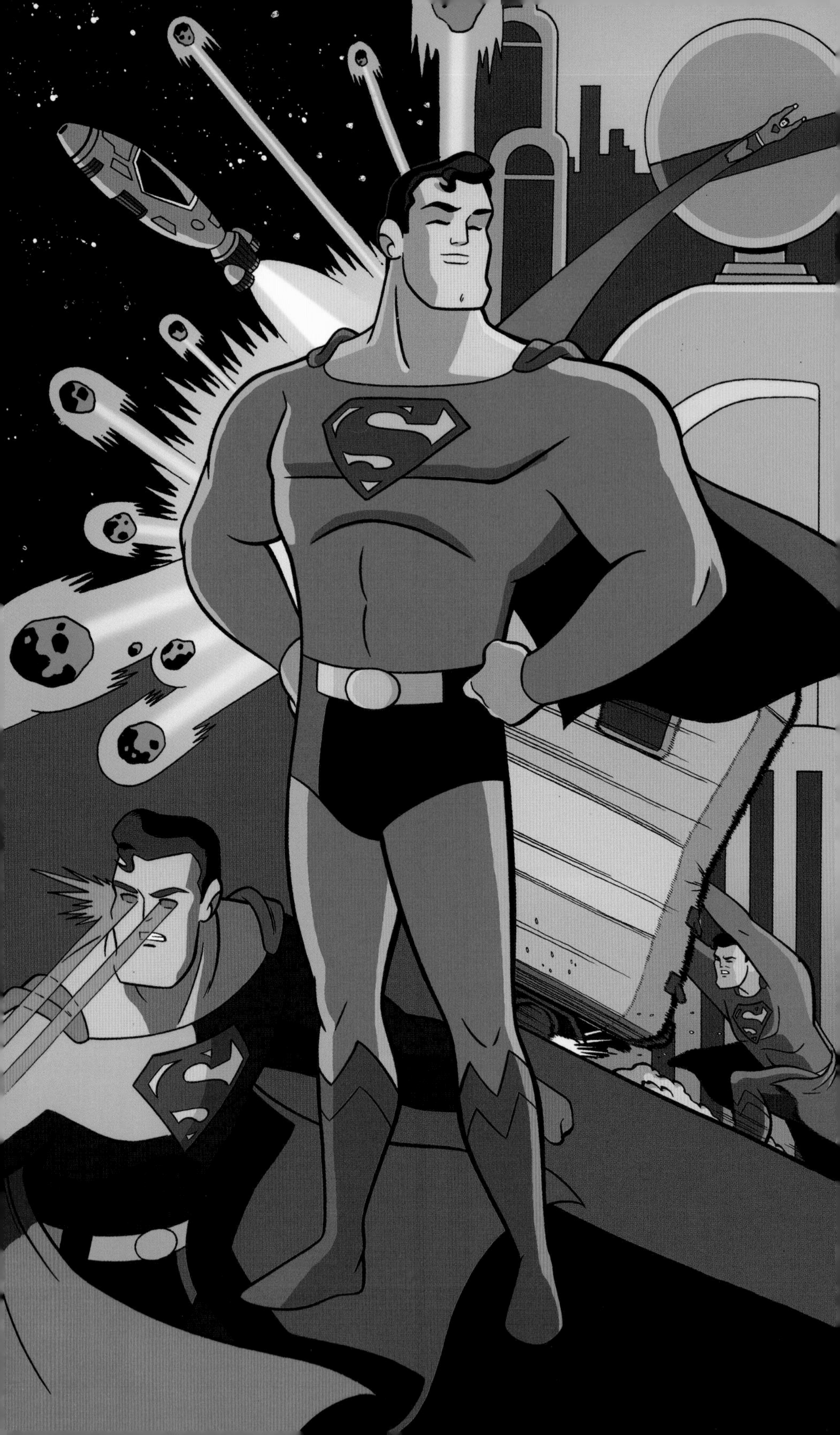

Born among the stars.
Raised on planet Earth.
With incredible powers,
he became the
World's Greatest Super Hero.
These are...

THE AMAZING ADVENTURES OF SUPERMAN!™

Chapter 1

POP GOES THE EVIL

Clark Kent sits at his

desk inside the Daily Planet

Building. The reporter stares

at a blank computer screen.

He waits for the next big

story to pop into his head.

Then . . . **POP! POP! POP!**

Suddenly, a loud popping

sound comes from outside

the building. Clark and the

others rush to the window.

"Look, up in the sky!"

says his boss, Perry White.

He points at a sparkling

globe above the buildings.

It's not a bird. Or a plane.

"A bubble!" Clark shouts.

Out of sight, Clark sheds
his thick glasses, suit, and
tie. He reveals the red and
blue uniform of his secret
identity: Superman!

The super hero quickly exits the Daily Planet Building and soars into sky. **FWOOOOSH!** He rockets toward the bubble trouble.

Chapter 2

BURST A BUBBLE

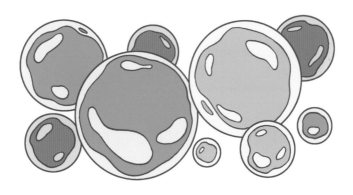

A split second later,

Superman nears the coast

of Metropolis. Dozens of

bubbles float over the bay,

drifting toward the city.

The giant bubbles are filled with thousands of gallons of ocean water. Whales, sharks, lobsters, and other sea creatures are trapped inside!

 **"HAHAHAHA!"** A robotic laugh echoes through the air. Superman looks at the bay. "Black Manta!" he says. The super-villain stands atop a high-tech machine on the surface of the ocean. The surrounding water boils like a pot of spaghetti. More bubbles float into the sky.

"What goes up must come down," Black Manta explains. "Soon, it'll be raining catfish and dogfish. The city will flood, and my kingdom will grow!"

Superman flies toward

one of the globes. "I hate to

burst your bubble, Manta,"

he begins, pulling back his

fist. "But I will anyway."

"Stop!" shouts a voice.

Aquaman splashes up from the bubbling bay. "Your super-strength may harm those sea creatures inside," he tells Superman.

"You're right, old pal," Superman agrees.

Aquaman notices a bubble floating in the breeze. "Don't worry," he adds. "You can still deliver the final blow!"

Chapter 3

DOWN WITH THE SHIP

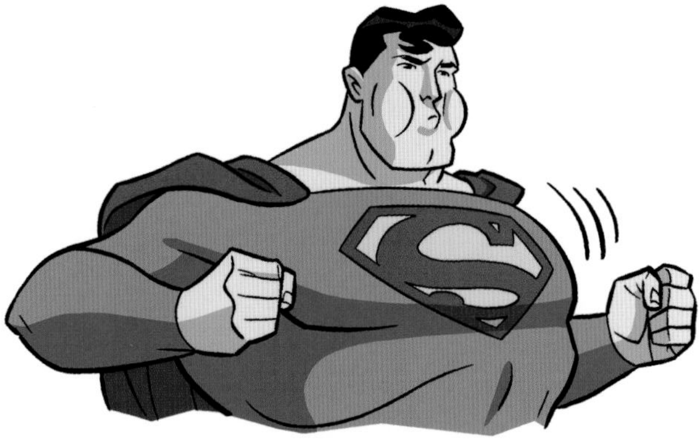

A quick plan later, Superman soars higher into the sky. The super hero takes in a deep breath. He fills his powerful lungs with air.

Superman blows down at the giant bubbles with his super-breath. The gust of wind sends the bubbles toward the water below.

Aquaman swims back and forth on the surface of the ocean. He raises his trident at the falling bubbles. POP! POP! POP!

The Sea King gently pops each bubble with the spear. Crab, coral, and sea turtles fall safely back into the sea.

"There's more where that came from!" shouts Manta.

The super-villain turns up the dial on a remote control. The bubble machine shakes beneath his feet. The ocean rumbles and spits.

More bubbles rise from the sea, faster and faster.

One bubble lifts a large, sunken fishing boat into the sky. The boat hovers above Black Manta and his bubble-making machine.

Superman thinks fast.

The super hero takes

another deep breath. This

time, he cools the air inside

his powerful lungs.

Superman blasts the

bubble with his freeze

breath. It

instantly

freezes.

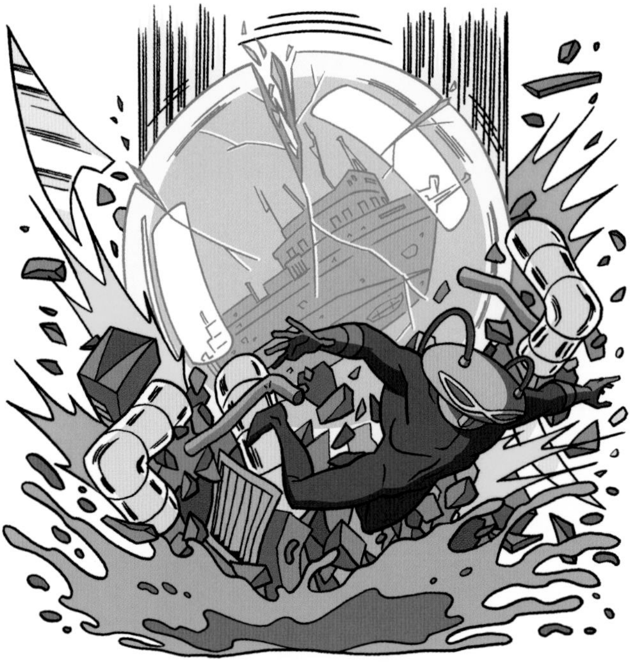

The bubble falls from the sky like a two-ton boulder. SMAAAAAAASH!

The icy bubble crashes down on Black Manta and his machine.

The bubble maker crumbles into the sea, and the waters calm.

"Looks like Black Manta went down with the ship," jokes Superman.

"Down but not out," adds Aquaman.

"Thanks for another amazing adventure, old pal!" says Superman.

A tiny bubble falls from the sky and lands on the tip of Aquaman's trident. POP!

"Sure thing," says the Sea King, smiling. "Call me again if anything pops up!"

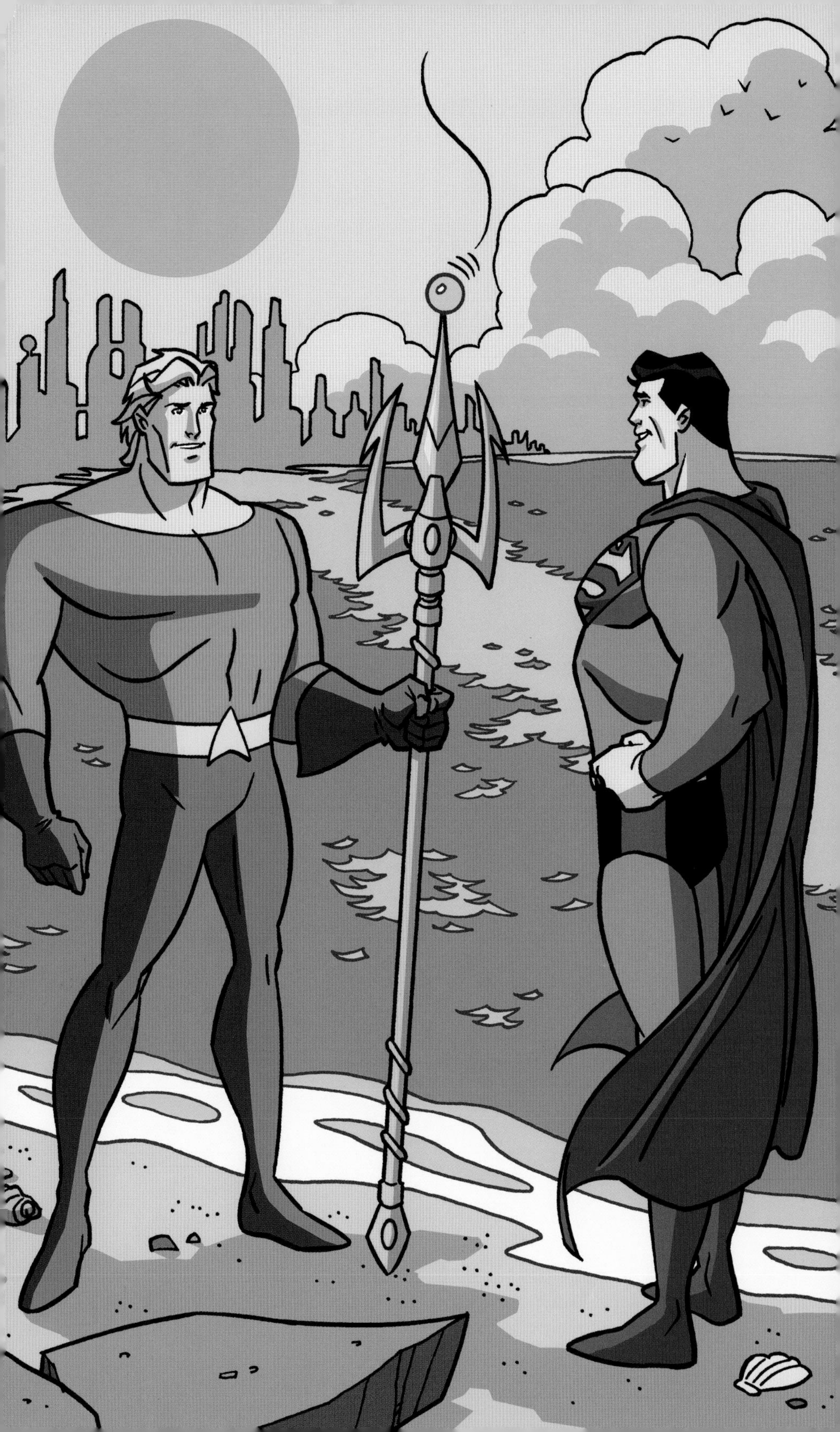

SUPERMAN'S SECRET MESSAGE!

Hey, kids! Which super hero protects the Seven Seas?

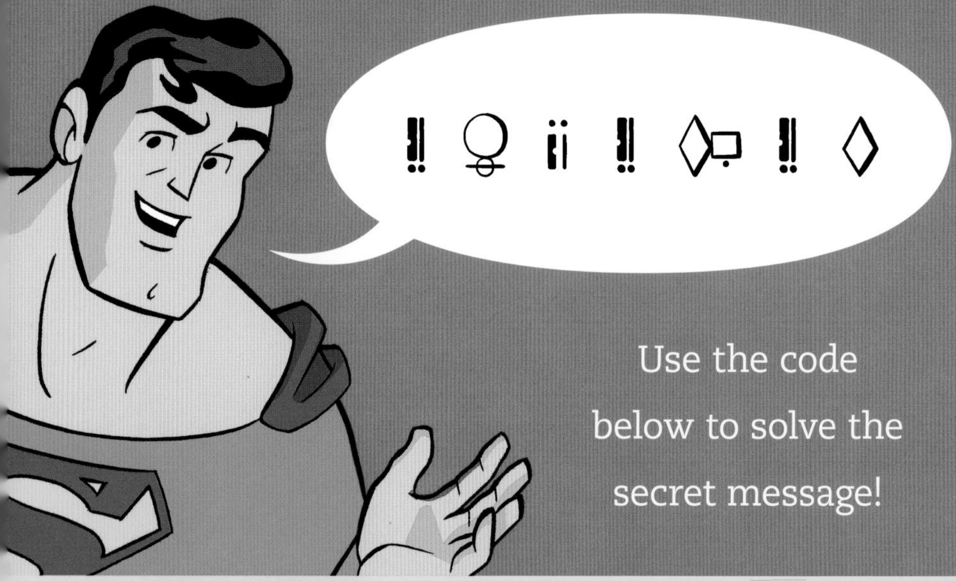

Use the code below to solve the secret message!

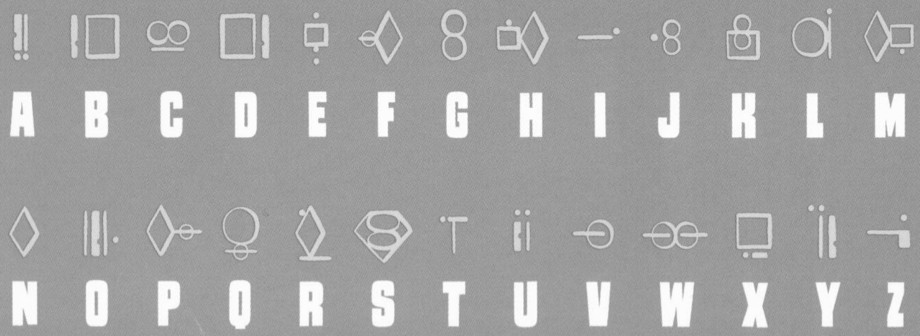
A B C D E F G H I J K L M
N O P Q R S T U V W X Y Z

globe (GLOHB) — anything shaped like a round ball

bay (BAY) — a portion of the ocean that is partly closed off by land

boulder (BOHL-dur) — a large, rounded rock

reporter (ri-POR-tur) — someone who gathers and reports the news

trident (TRYE-duhnt) — a spear with three prongs

uniform (YOO-nuh-form) — a special set of clothes worn by a super hero

THE AMAZING ADVENTURES OF SUPERMAN!™

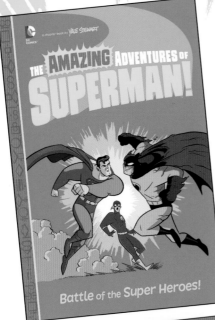

DC COMICS
a chapter book by YALE STEWART
THE AMAZING ADVENTURES OF SUPERMAN!
Battle of the Super Heroes!

DC COMICS
a chapter book by YALE STEWART
THE AMAZING ADVENTURES OF SUPERMAN!
Escape from Future World!

DC COMICS
a chapter book by YALE STEWART
THE AMAZING ADVENTURES OF SUPERMAN!
Alien Superman!

DC COMICS
a chapter book by YALE STEWART
THE AMAZING ADVENTURES OF SUPERMAN!
Creatures from Planet X!

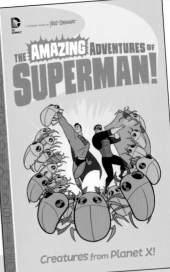

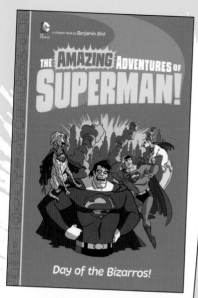

Day of the Bizarros!

Supergirl's Pet Problem!

Bubble Trouble!

Magic Monsters!

Author
Benjamin Bird is a children's book editor and writer from St. Paul, Minnesota. He has written books about some of today's most popular characters, including Batman, Superman, Wonder Woman, Scooby-Doo, Tom & Jerry, and more.

Illustrator
Tim Levins is best known for his work on the Eisner Award-winning DC Comics series Batman: Gotham Adventures. Tim has illustrated other DC titles, such as Justice League Adventures and Batgirl. He enjoys life in Midland, Ontario, Canada, with his wife, son, dog, and two horses.